Written by
John Kendrick Bangs

Illustrated by
Frank Sofo

 Ideals Children's Books • Nashville, Tennessee
an imprint of Hambleton-Hill Publishing, Inc.

To my wife, for her love and support, and to the memory of John Gundelfinger.

— Frank Sofo

Published by Ideals Children's Books
An imprint of Hambleton-Hill Publishing, Inc.
1501 County Hospital Road
Nashville, Tennessee 37218

Library of Congress Cataloging-in-Publication Data
Bangs, John Kendrick, 1862-1922.
The Time Shop / by John Kendrick Bangs ; illustrated by Frank Sofo. — 1st ed.
p.   cm.
Summary: Bobby takes a journey to the Time Shop, where goods are purchased with days, hours, and minutes, and buys a gift
for his mother after learning an important lesson from Procrastination, the thief of time.
ISBN 1-57102-137-X (hardcover)
[1. Time—Fiction. 2. Conduct of life—Fiction.] I. Sofo, Frank, ill. II. Title.
PZ7.B225T 1998
[Fic]—dc2198-16587

CIP

AC

First Edition

The illustrations in this book were rendered in acrylic.
The text type is set in Garamond Light Condensed.

Cover and book design by
LaughlinStudio

Dost thou love life?
Then do not squander time,
for that's the stuff that life is made of.

—*Benjamin Franklin*

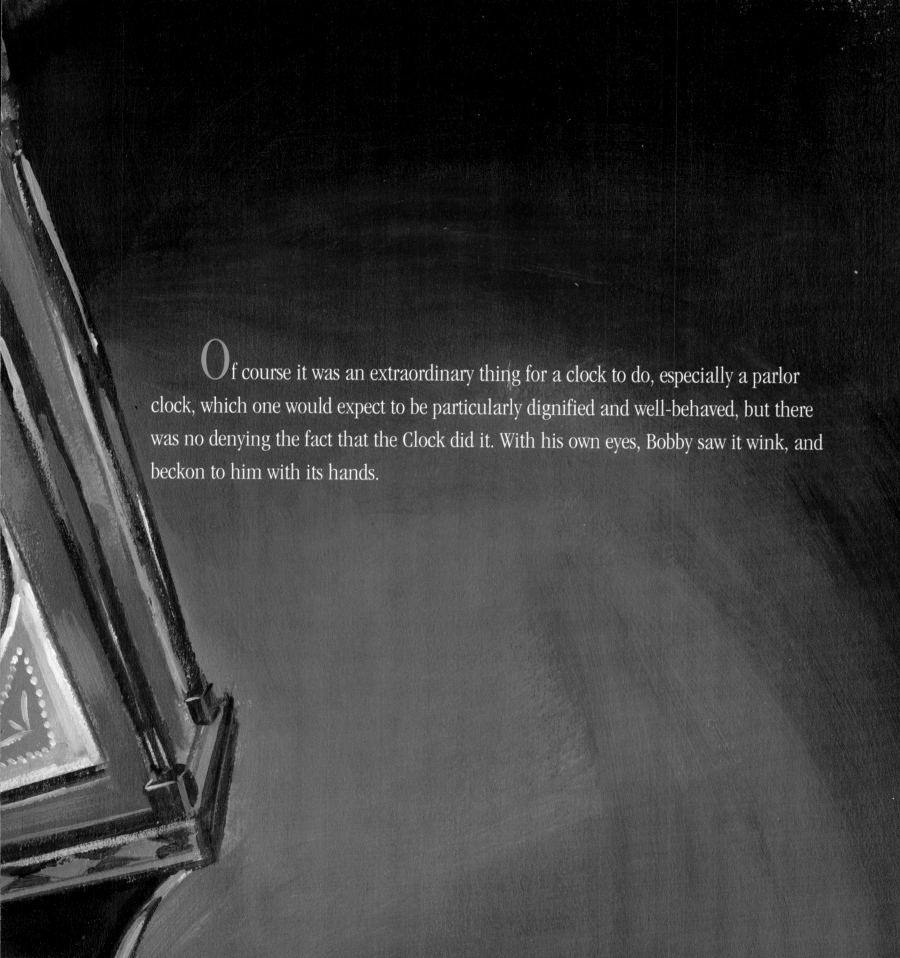

Of course it was an extraordinary thing for a clock to do, especially a parlor clock, which one would expect to be particularly dignified and well-behaved, but there was no denying the fact that the Clock did it. With his own eyes, Bobby saw it wink, and beckon to him with its hands.

To be sure, Bobby had never noticed that the Clock had eyes or fingers on its hands to beckon with. As he lay stretched out along the rug in front of the great open fireplace, he looked up curiously at the Clock's now smiling face. In a whisper, he asked, "Are you beckoning to me?"

"Of course I am," replied the Clock, in a soft, silvery tone, somewhat like the tinkling of a bell. "You didn't think I was beckoning to the piano, did you?"

"But what did you want with me?"

"Well," replied the Clock, "I am beginning to feel a bit run down. I thought I'd go over to the shop and get a little more time to keep me going. Christmas is coming soon, and everybody is so impatient for its arrival that I don't want to slow down and have all the children blame me for its lateness."

"What shop are you going to?" asked Bobby, interested at once, for he was very fond of shops and shopping.

"Why, the Time Shop, of course," said the Clock. "We clocks have to get our supply of time from there or we couldn't keep going."

"I don't think I understand," said Bobby, with a puzzled look on his face. "What is a Time Shop, and what do they sell there?"

"Oh, anything from a bunch of bananas or a barrel of sawdust up to an automobile," returned the Clock. "What they've got in the Time Shop depends entirely upon what you want. I thought that having nothing to do for a little while but look at those flames trying to learn to dance, you might like to go with me and visit the old shop. Maybe you can spend a little time there whilst I am laying in a fresh supply to keep me on the move."

"I'd love to go," said Bobby eagerly.

"Very well, then," returned the Clock. "Close your eyes, count seventeen backward, then open your eyes again, and you will see what you will see."

Bobby shut his eyes and counted from seventeen back to one with a rapidity that would have surprised even his teacher. He opened his eyes again and looked around, and what he saw—well, that was more extraordinary than ever!

Instead of standing on the parlor rug before the fireplace, he found himself in the broadest aisle of the ground floor of a huge department store. It was infinitely larger than any store he had ever seen before, and oh, dear me, how dreadfully crowded it was! The crowd of Christmas shoppers that Bobby remembered to have seen last year was as nothing to that which thronged this wonderful place.

"Look, Bobby," said the Clock, "how dreadfully hurried some of these poor shoppers appear to be, and how wistfully some of them gaze at the fine bargains to be seen here, which either because they have not saved it, or have wasted it, they have not time to buy! I shall not be long Bobby, please enjoy your look around!"

With this, the Clock turned and made off to the supply shop, leaving Bobby to stare in wonder at all the splendid offerings on the shelves and counters of the Time Shop.

"Well, young man," said a kindly supervisor, pausing in his majestic march up the aisle, "what can we do for you today?"

"Nothing, thank you, sir," said Bobby. "I have just come to look around."

"Ah!" said the gentleman with a look of disappointment on his face. "I should think that a boy like you would be able to decide what he really wanted and go directly to the proper department and get it."

"Got any bicycles?" asked Bobby, seizing upon the first thing that entered his mind.

"Best there are! Step this way please." He turned to an older gentleman standing nearby and said, "Mr. Promptness, will you be so good as to show this young man our line of bicycles?" Then, turning to Bobby, he added, "To encourage business we like to see that newcomers have a chance to avail themselves of the opportunities of the shop, so here are a few time-pieces with which you can buy what you want."

The kindly supervisor handed Bobby twenty round golden coins, twenty silver, and twenty copper ones. Each was about the size of a nickel, and all were as bright as if they had just been minted.

"The golden pieces, my boy, are days. The silver ones are hours, and the coppers are minutes. I hope you will use them wisely, and find your visit to our shop so enjoyable that you will become a regular customer."

With this, the supervisor moved along to direct a gray-haired gentleman with a great store of years in his possession to the place where he could make the last payment on a stock of wisdom. Bobby was left with Mr. Promptness, the salesman, who immediately showed him all the bicycles they had in stock.

"This is a pretty good one for a boy your age," said Mr. Promptness as he gave the bicycle a push along the top of the mahogany counter. It pirouetted a couple of times on its hind wheel, and then gracefully turning, rolled back to Mr. Promptness.

"How much is that?" asked Bobby.

"Sixteen hours and forty-five minutes," said Mr. Promptness. "It used to be a twenty-five hour bicycle, but we have marked everything down this season. Everybody is so rushed these days that very few people have any spare time to spend."

"Sixteen hours and forty-five minutes?" asked Bobby. "How much is that in dollars?"

"We don't do business in dollars here, my lad," said he. "This is the Time Shop, and what you buy you buy with time: days, hours, minutes, and seconds."

"I should think that you would rather do business for money," said Bobby.

"No, no, my son," said Mr. Promptness. "Time is a far better possession than money. It often will buy things that money couldn't possibly purchase."

"Then I must be rich," said Bobby. "I've got no end of time. Seems to me sometimes that I've got all the time there is."

"Well," said Mr. Promptness, "you must remember that its value depends entirely upon how you use it. Time thrown away or wasted is of no value at all. Where do you get your clothes, your food, your playthings?" asked the salesman.

"Oh, my parents get all those things for me," returned Bobby.

"Well, they have to pay for them," said Mr. Promptness, "and they have to pay for them in time, too. Do you spend yours well?"

"Sometimes," said Bobby, "and sometimes I just waste it." He went on: "You see, Mr. Promptness, I didn't know there was a Time Shop where you could buy such beautiful things, but now that I do, you will find me here often, spending what I have on things worth having."

"I hope so," said Mr. Promptness, patting Bobby affectionately on the shoulder. "How much have you got with you now?"

"Only these," said Bobby, jingling the time in his pocket. "Of course, next week when my Christmas holiday begins I shall have a lot—three whole weeks—that's twenty-one days, you know."

"Well, you can only count on what you have in hand, but from the sound in your pocket I fancy you can have the bicycle if you want it," said Mr. Promptness.

"How much is that electric train over there?" asked Bobby excitedly.

"That's rather expensive," Mr. Promptness replied. "It will cost you two weeks, three days, ten minutes, and thirty seconds."

"Humph," said Bobby. "I guess that's a little too much for me." Suddenly an idea flashed across his mind. "There is one thing I want very much, Mr. Promptness. I'd like to buy a Christmas present for my mother, if I can get a nice one with the time I've got."

"About how much would you like to spend on it?" asked Mr. Promptness, with a soft light in his eye.

"Oh, I'd like to spend four or five years on it," said Bobby excitedly.

"That's very nice of you," said the salesman. "Why, I have known boys to give their mothers presents bought at this shop that were worth years, but which haven't cost them more than two or three hours because they made up the difference in love."

Mr. Promptness reached up to a long shelf and brought down a little card, framed in gold, and illustrated with a lovely picture that seemed to Bobby to be the prettiest thing he had ever seen.

"This is a little thing that was written long ago," said Mr. Promptness, "by a man who spent much time in this shop. Thousands of people have been made happier by the way he spent his hours. He put a tremendous lot of love into all that he did. His name was Thackeray. Read this and tell me what you think of it," said Mr. Promptness.

He handed Bobby the beautiful card, and the little fellow, taking it in his hand, read the sentence:

"You see, my dear little boy," said the kindly salesman, "that is worth—oh, I don't know how many years! Your mother, I am sure, would rather know that is how you feel about her, than have you give her the finest jewels that we have to sell. And how much do you think we charge for it?"

"Forty years!" gasped Bobby.

"No," replied Mr. Promptness. "Five minutes. Shall we put it aside for you?"

"Yes, indeed," cried Bobby, delighted to have so beautiful a Christmas gift for his mother.

They walked down the aisles of the great shop, looking at the many things that time well expended would buy. Bobby paused for a moment and spent two minutes on a glass of lemonade and purchased a quarter of an hour's worth of peanuts to share with Mr. Promptness.

Soon, they came to a number of large rooms at one end of the shop, and in one of these Bobby saw quite a gathering of youngsters somewhat older than himself. Not one of them seemed to be wasting even an instant, as they were very busy pouring over huge books, and writing things down in little notebooks.

"These young people are buying an education with their time," said Mr. Promptness. "They come here and spend their time on the things we have in our library. It is an interesting fact that what is bought in this room can never be stolen from you, and it happens more often than not that when they have spent hundreds of hours in here they win more time to spend on the other things that we have on sale. But there are others, I am sorry to say, who stop on their way here in the morning and fritter their loose change away in the Shop of Idleness across the way—a minute here, a half hour there, and when they arrive here they haven't got enough left to buy a thing."

"What can you buy at the Shop of Idleness?" asked Bobby, going to the street door and looking across the way at the shop in question, which seemed, indeed, to be doing a considerable business, if one could judge from the crowds within.

"Oh, a little fun," said Mr. Promptness. "But not the real, genuine kind, my boy. It is sort of imitation fun that looks like the real thing, but on close inspection turns out to be nothing but frivolity."

"Who is that pleasant-looking gentleman just outside the door?" asked Bobby.

"He is the general manager of the Shop of Idleness," said the salesman. "As you say, he is a pleasant-looking fellow, but you must beware of him, Bobby. He is not a good person to have around. He is a very active businessman and his business is to rob his customers of all their time."

Mr. Promptness' words were interrupted by his rival across the way, who, observing Bobby standing in the doorway, cleverly tossed one of his cards across the street so that it fell at the little boy's feet. Bobby stooped down, picked it up, and read:

THE SHOP OF IDLENESS
PROCRASTINATION,
General Manager.
Put Off Everything And Visit Our Shop.

"So, he's Procrastination, is he?" said Bobby, looking at the man with interest, for he had heard his father speak of him.

"Yes, and he is truly what they say he is," said Mr. Promptness. "They call him the thief of time."

Now it is a peculiarity of Procrastination that he has very sharp ears, and he can hear a great many things that you wouldn't think could travel so far, and, as Bobby spoke, Procrastination turned suddenly and with a wave of his hand, came running across the street.

Mr. Promptness seized Bobby by the arm and pulled him into the Time Shop, but not quickly enough, for he was unable to close the door before his rival was at their side.

"Glad to see you, my boy," said Procrastination, handing him another card. "Come on over to my place. It's much easier to find what you want, and we've got a lot of comfortable chairs in which to sit and think things over. You needn't buy anything today, just come in and look around."

"Don't listen to him, Bobby," said Mr. Promptness, anxiously whispering in the boy's ear. "He will pick your pocket if you let him come close. Come along with me and see the things we keep on the upper floors. I am sure they will please you."

"Going up!" cried the elevator boy.

"Come, Bobby," said Mr. Promptness in a beseeching tone.

"All aboard!" cried the elevator boy.

"I'll be there in two seconds," returned Bobby.

"Can't wait!" cried the elevator boy as he banged the iron door shut. The car shot to the upper regions where the keepers of the Time Shop kept their most beautiful things.

"Too bad," said Mr. Promptness, shaking his head sadly. "Now, Procrastination," he added fiercely, "I must ask you to leave this shop."

"Tutt-tutt-tutt, my dear Mr. Promptness!" retorted Procrastination, still looking dangerously pleasant, and smiling as if it must all be a joke. "This shop of yours is a public place, sir, and I have just as much right to spend my time here as anybody else."

"Very well, sir," said Mr. Promptness, "but you will please remember that I warned you to go."

Mr. Promptness turned as he spoke and touched a button on the back of the counter, which immediately called forth a terrific and deafening clanging of bells. At that exact moment from upstairs and down came rushing all the forces of time. They fell upon the unwelcome visitor, thrust him into the street, and promptly barred and bolted the doors against his return.

"Mercy me!" cried Bobby's friend the Clock, rushing up just as the door was slammed to. "What's the meaning of all this uproar?"

"Nothing," said Mr. Promptness. "Only that wicked old Procrastination again. He caught sight of Bobby here—"

"I only stopped a minute to say hello to him," explained Bobby, sheepishly.

"Well, I'm sorry that you made his acquaintance," said the Clock, "but come along. It's getting late and we're due back home. Have you paid your bill?"

"Here it is Bobby. I think you will find it correct," said Mr. Promptness.

Bobby looked over the items and saw that the total due was three days, four hours, and fifty minutes, well within the value of the time he had been given, but alas, when he put his hand in his pocket to get the coins, they were gone. Not even a minute was left! Procrastination had succeeded only too well.

"Very sorry, Bobby," said Mr. Promptness, "although I warned you against that fellow, I feel sorry enough for you to help a little. I'll give you five minutes, my boy, to pay for the little card for your mother's Christmas present."

Bobby started to thank Mr. Promptness for his generosity, but there was no chance for this. Suddenly, Bobby felt himself being shaken and whirled around and around. Terrified, he closed his eyes for an instant. When he opened them again he found himself back on the parlor rug, lying in front of the fire, his father shaking him gently.

Bobby glanced up to see what had become of the Clock, but the grouchy old ticker stared solemnly ahead, with its hands pointed sternly at eight o'clock, which meant Bobby had to go to bed at once.

"Please let me stay up just ten minutes longer," pleaded Bobby.

"No, sir," replied his father. "No more procrastination son—trot along."

And it seemed to Bobby as he walked out of the room that that saucy old Clock grinned.

Incidentally, in the whirl of his return, Bobby lost the card that the good Mr. Promptness had given him for his mother, but the little fellow remembered the words, and when Christmas morning came his mother found them painted in watercolors on a piece of cardboard by Bobby's own hand. When she read them a tear of happiness came into her eyes, and she hugged the little chap and thanked him for the most beautiful Christmas present she had ever received.

And there was no mistaking the confused look on his mother's face as he said, "It isn't so very valuable though, Mother. It only cost two hours and a half, and I know where you can get a better looking one in a gold frame for only five minutes!"